W9-AMB-575

DiNKiN DiNGS

AND THE

DOUBLE FROM DIMENSION 9

To Jane, Tom, Lauren, and everyone at Stripes for always
going the extra mile and beyond! ~ GB

To little Leni Frances and her great-grandma Corke ~ PW

Check out Dinkin's Bebo page at:
www.bebo.com/dinkindings

GROSSET & DUNLAP
Published by the Penguin Group
Penguin Group (USA) Inc., 375 Hudson Street, New York, New York 10014, USA
Penguin Group (Canada), 90 Eglinton Avenue East, Suite 700, Toronto, Ontario M4P 2Y3,
Canada (a division of Pearson Penguin Canada Inc.)
Penguin Books Ltd., 80 Strand, London WC2R 0RL, England
Penguin Group Ireland, 25 St. Stephen's Green, Dublin 2, Ireland
(a division of Penguin Books Ltd.)
Penguin Group (Australia), 250 Camberwell Road, Camberwell, Victoria 3124,
Australia (a division of Pearson Australia Group Pty. Ltd.)
Penguin Books India Pvt. Ltd., 11 Community Centre, Panchsheel Park,
New Delhi – 110 017, India
Penguin Group (NZ), 67 Apollo Drive, Rosedale, North Shore 0632, New Zealand
(a division of Pearson New Zealand Ltd.)
Penguin Books (South Africa) (Pty.) Ltd., 24 Sturdee Avenue, Rosebank,
Johannesburg 2196, South Africa
Penguin Books Ltd., Registered Offices: 80 Strand, London WC2R 0RL, England

Text copyright © 2010 Guy Bass. Illustrations copyright © 2010 Pete Williamson. Published
in Great Britain in 2010 by Stripes Publishing. First published in the United States in 2011
by Grosset & Dunlap, a division of Penguin Young Readers Group, 345 Hudson Street,
New York, New York 10014. GROSSET & DUNLAP is a trademark of
Penguin Group (USA) Inc. Printed in the U.S.A.

Library of Congress Cataloging-in-Publication Data is available.

ISBN 978-0-448-45433-7 (pbk)   10 9 8 7 6 5 4 3 2 1
ISBN 978-0-448-45434-4 (HC)   10 9 8 7 6 5 4 3 2 1

Dinkin Dings

AND THE DOUBLE FROM DIMENSION 9

GUY BASS

illustrated by
PETE WILLIAMSON

Grosset & Dunlap
An Imprint of Penguin Group (USA) Inc.

THE PROBLEM WITH DINKIN DINGS

Dinkin Dings was afraid of everything. And not just actual scary things, like being flushed down a man-eating toilet or fired out of a giant cannon into an alligator-filled wading pool. No, he was afraid of pretty much completely and totally everything.

Well, almost everything. There were just three things Dinkin wasn't afraid of:

1. The monster under his bed
2. The skeleton in his closet
3. The ghost outside his window

In fact, they were his best friends.

He called them The Frightening Things.

PARK PERIL

Time: 10:22 AM
Temperature: 73.4°F
Terror: 7,694 scariness pounds

"Dinkin, your dad's back—it's time to go!" shouted Dinkin's mom from downstairs.

"Go without me!" cried Dinkin from his bed. Two point nine seconds later he heard the sound of footsteps stomping angrily up the stairs. He pulled his blanket up to his chin just as his mother pushed open the door.

"What on earth are you doing back in bed?" asked Mrs. Dings.

"I'm—I'm sick!" replied Dinkin. "Don't get too close, I'm highly contagious!"

"That's funny, you were okay two

minutes ago," said Mrs. Dings suspiciously. "In fact, you were perfectly fine before I mentioned the idea of going to the park."

"It's Purple Fungus Fever . . . the tropical kind!" said Dinkin, wiping his brow. "I don't know how long I've got left . . ."

"Dinkin, I told you as soon as your father got back from the optometrist, we were going to the park, and we are—purple fungus or no purple fungus," said Mrs. Dings, which made Dinkin worry that he might *actually* have Purple Fungus Fever. "It is a lovely, sunny day. It is a Sunday. This is what families do on lovely, sunny Sundays."

"You can't take me to the park!" screamed Dinkin. "I'm too young to die!"

Dinkin had always been afraid of parks. Aside from all the obvious, titanic terrors (grass, trees, ponds, people, etc.), parks were riddled with hidden horrors. Dinkin's top five park fears were:

1) Prehistoric Monster Attack (According to Dinkin, tree-rannosauruses had been hiding in trees for millions of years. Parks were especially tree-rannosaurus friendly as they offered plenty of passing snacks in the shape of children looking for their lost Frisbees.)

2) Tidal Waves

3) Tornadoes

4) Tornado-Waves
(half wet, half windy, all
terrifying)

5) Superpsychotic Robo-
Poodles (Specifically the
Mark 7 model, which look
exactly like a normal poodle
but include the Atomic Yap
upgrade.)

"Oh, Dinkin, you're just being silly again. Now, get out of bed this minute," said Mrs. Dings impatiently as she pulled back Dinkin's blanket. "Oh, Dinkin! Is that your *bike lock*?" she cried. Sure enough, Dinkin's right arm was chained to his headboard with a bicycle lock.

"Actually, it's my Personal Peril Prevention Padlock," said Dinkin proudly.

"Dinkin Danger Dings," said Mrs. Dings (using Dinkin's full name to show she meant business), "I'm only going to ask you once— where is the key to that lock?"

Dinkin shrugged and let out an involuntary burp.

"*Please* don't tell me you ate it . . . " sighed his mom.

HIDDEN DANGER DETECTION GLASSES

Hacksaw hazard: 3,256 scariness pounds

Tree-rannosaurus terror: 6,455 scariness pounds

Peeved parent peril: 8,893 scariness pounds

12 It took seventeen minutes of prodding with a metal coat hanger for Mrs. Dings to open the Personal Peril Prevention Padlock. As Dinkin frequently chained himself to things to get out of doing scary stuff, his mom had become quite a skillful lock-picker. By the time she popped the lock, Mr. Dings was poking his head around the door.

"Well? What do you think of my glasses?" he said, tapping his new eyewear. Dinkin was immediately nervous. Who knew what terrifyingly sinister purpose these new glasses served? At the very least, they seemed to have long-range laser lenses!

"Very stylish, Mr. Dings," said Mrs. Dings. "And now that you're back, there's nothing to stop us from going to the park . . . right, Dinkin? So get out of those pajamas and into some clothes."

"But—," began Dinkin.

"And no *buts*!" said his mother.

13

The trip to the park seemed to take forever, giving Dinkin plenty of time to panic about what horrifying fate awaited him. His mother had pushed him into the car so quickly that he had no time to pack his Tornado-Trapping Trousers, his poodle-paralyzing Drowsy Dog Device, or his long-range Dino-Discoverer. By the time they arrived at the park, Dinkin was beside himself with fear.

14 "AAA-AAAH!" he screamed as his mother prodded him out of the car. "Look at all the unseen dangers! We're doomed! Doomed!"

"Dinkin, how can you be worried about something if you can't even see it?" said Mrs. Dings. "Can't you at least wait until we're attacked by tree-rannosauruses before you panic?"

"But by then it'll be too late!" yelled Dinkin. "Danger is everywhere!"

"Actually, Dink, there is a way to check for hidden dangers," said Mr. Dings, taking off his glasses and winking at Mrs. Dings. "A special, secret way. In fact, it's really the *only* way to know for sure . . . But no, you're probably not interested."

"What do you mean? Of course I'm interested!" screamed Dinkin. "Tell me, quick, before the tornado-wave comes!"

"Well, okay, but keep it to yourself or everyone will want a pair," said Mr. Dings, holding out his glasses. "It's *these*."

15

"Your new glasses?" said Dinkin and Mrs. Dings together.

"Glasses? These aren't glasses!" laughed Mr. Dings. "They just *look* like glasses so as not to arouse suspicion. These are my, uh, *Hidden Danger Detection Glasses*."

"Hidden . . . Danger . . . Detection Glasses?" repeated Dinkin slowly.

"I didn't know they'd started selling those at the optometrist's . . . ," giggled Mrs. Dings.

"Well, I had to pay extra, of course, but it was worth it," said Mr. Dings. "The Hidden Danger Detection Glasses reveal every scary thing that's nearby, however well hidden. Anything even slightly unnerving shows up as clear as day!"

"And they . . . they really work?" said Dinkin, wondering why on earth his dad hadn't mentioned them before.

"Oh, yes! These are top of the line. I've just had a thorough scan of the park and we seem to be in the clear. Not one hidden danger in sight. Here, you try them," said Mr. Dings, handing his glasses to Dinkin. Every instinct told Dinkin to be suspicious of them . . . but what if they really did work? He wanted more than anything to know *exactly* what scariness surrounded him. Slowly, with uncertainty, he put on the glasses.

"Everything looks . . . the same," he said, almost disappointed. "And a bit blurry."

"Exactly! That's because there isn't any scariness here! The blurriness just means everything is . . . extra safe. Lucky for us, huh?" said his dad.

Dinkin looked around, paying close attention to the trees, clouds, and any passing poodles. The Hidden Danger Detection Glasses didn't reveal anything! Not one even slightly terrifying concealed horror. Dinkin turned even paler than normal.

"Are you all right, Dinkin?" asked his mom.

"I don't know—I feel a bit . . . funny," answered a confused Dinkin.

"Do you know what I think? I think maybe you don't feel as scared," smiled Mr. Dings.

"Not . . . scared?" whispered Dinkin, peering into the sky to make sure there were no signs of tornado-waves. "Maybe . . ."

Mr. and Mrs. Dings looked a little amazed, and then wide, delighted smiles spread across their faces.

"So," said Mr. Dings, "now what?"

FEAR-FREE

Chances of the cat from across the street actually being a Secret Saber-Toothed Cyber-Tiger from Somewhere near Saturn: 0.00002%
Chances of Dinkin's dresser actually being man-eating: 0.0001%
Chances of there being nothing actually scary in this chapter at all: 0%

Dinkin and his parents spent the next two hours having what normal people living normal lives might describe as "a nice time." Thanks to the Hidden Danger Detection Glasses, Dinkin could constantly scan the park for concealed menaces, but oddly, the glasses didn't reveal anything terrifying at all. For the first time since he could remember, Dinkin had nothing to be scared of. He found himself with a lot of time on his hands, and no idea how to spend it.

"Hey, Dinkin, want to wander down to that little pond over there?" asked Mr. Dings, pointing to a shallow pool full of swimming children.

"What? Are you crazy? There could be anything in there! Mutated mer-monsters, buckets of brain-melting toxic ooze, even a whole school of vampiranhas!"

"Well, check with the glasses—then you can know for sure," replied his dad.

Dinkin peered through the glasses at the pond, sure that there would be some horrifying horrors hiding beneath the water. But it just looked like a pond—tranquil, quiet, and more than a little inviting.

"No hidden dangers," said Dinkin.

"Great! Let's get in and swim!" said Mr. Dings.

"S-s-swim?" squeaked Dinkin.

"Sure, what's there to be afraid of?"

laughed Mr. Dings, taking off his shoes and socks and rolling up his pant legs. Dinkin watched his dad rush down to the pond and splash around like a three-year-old. Slowly, Dinkin began to creep toward the water.

"I don't believe it . . . ," whispered Mrs. Dings as Dinkin stood on the edge of the water. A moment later, he took off his shoes and socks, and stuck in a toe. And so it was that for the first time in his life, Dinkin Dings actually *swam* . . .

without screaming even once.

As they drove back to the house after an almost panic-free afternoon, Mr. and Mrs. Dings couldn't believe that the solution to Dinkin's fear of everything might be as simple as a pair of glasses. He'd never seemed so un-terrified!

Dinkin just stared out the car window at the normally terrifying world outside. Finally he said, "It's weird, though . . . in all this time, the Hidden Danger Detection Glasses haven't shown *anything* terrifying at all."

"Well, Dink," smiled his dad. "Maybe the world's not as scary as you thought."

As it happened, when they got home, Dinkin spotted three things that would have normally made him scream in terror:

1) MISS WHISKERS (THE CAT FROM ACROSS THE STREET) — or as Dinkin knew her, the Secret Saber-Toothed Cyber-Tiger from Somewhere near Saturn

2) A LADYBUG — part lady, part bug . . . disguised as a beetle

3) HIS BICYCLE — It had been sitting on the front porch since Dinkin had gotten it for his birthday. Dinkin was absolutely convinced that his bike had been taken over by the Wheeliens — power-hungry Alien Invaders who used their ability to control bicycles to try and conquer the galaxy.

But the Hidden Danger Detection Glasses assured him that there was nothing to worry about. Dinkin had been fear-free for a total of three hours and forty-nine minutes, and he had to admit that it felt pretty good.

"Hey, Dink, why don't you hang on to those glasses?" said his dad, smiling at Mrs. Dings. "I'm happy to wear my old pair for now. It's worth it for a bit of peace and quiet."

"Really? Thanks!" said Dinkin as his mom and dad hugged for no reason whatsoever. Dinkin shrugged and made his way upstairs, anxious to check his room for concealed dangers. When he pushed open the door and looked around, he saw:

a table (just a plain, old table)

a dresser (clearly not man-eating)

a mirror (definitely not a doorway to another dimension)

Dinkin breathed a sigh of relief. It was as if, with the glasses, he didn't have to be scared of anything at all! He stepped confidently into his room and caught sight of his reflection in the mirror. The Hidden Danger Detection Glasses made him look really different, especially since everything was a little blurred. Dinkin took off the glasses and rubbed his eyes. After a moment he looked back at his reflection, but something didn't look right. After 1.3 seconds he realized what it was . . .

His reflection was still wearing glasses.

DOORWAY TO DIMENSION 9

Soda at 87% flatness
Cookies at 72.6% sogginess
Terror at 8,779 scariness pounds

"**AA-AAAA-AAAAH!**" screamed Dinkin in horror, dropping the glasses and running out of the room! "Mom, Dad, help!"

"What is it? What's going on?" said Dinkin's dad as Dinkin raced downstairs and into the kitchen. "Hey, why did you take off your glasses?"

"D-d-danger!" squealed Dinkin. "There was . . . There was someone in my mirror! A duplicate! A double! He looked exactly like me, except he was wearing glasses!"

"Oh, Dink, that's just your reflection, you

silly dilly," chuckled Mr. Dings. "You must have been wearing your glasses when you looked in the mirror!"

"I'd taken them off!" cried Dinkin, diving under the table. "It wasn't my reflection, it was a double . . . a dark, doom-bringing double from Dimension 9!"

"Dimension 9?" asked Mrs. Dings.

"The same-but-different dimension! Where everything looks like normal but is different in a million, menacing ways!" cried Dinkin. "Don't tell me you haven't heard of Dimension 9?"

"I didn't even know about dimensions one to eight," sighed Mrs. Dings.

It took two hours and fifty-five seconds for Mr. and Mrs. Dings to convince Dinkin that the only way to *really* know for sure whether his reflection was a double from Dimension 9 was to take another look. Against his better judgment, Dinkin found himself back in front of his mirror, with his eyes closed tight. His parents stood on either side of the mirror, making encouraging noises.

"There is nothing to be afraid of, I promise—just take a peek," said his mom.

Dinkin crossed his fingers, wished it was after midnight (so that The Frightening Things could be terrified alongside him), and looked in the mirror.

"It's . . . me," he whispered, seeing his reflection staring back at him. There wasn't a pair of glasses in sight.

"You see? There is no double from Dimension . . . wherever," said Mrs. Dings. "Now, we've had a nice day. Why don't we end the day with some cookies and soda?"

"Can the cookies be soaked in water to reduce the choking hazard?" asked Dinkin nervously. "And can the soda be flat to decrease brain-fizz?"

"Absolutely," smiled Mrs. Dings. She picked up the glasses and put them on the table. "You keep these for now, just in case. We'll see you downstairs when you're ready."

And with that, Mr. and Mrs. Dings made their way downstairs, leaving Dinkin alone. He felt so much better—there *was* no double from Dimension 9 . . . he was safe! He smiled and looked at himself in the mirror, one last time.

"Looks like it wasn't such a scary day, after all," he said, staring at his reflection.

"Don't be too sure," replied his reflection, and put its glasses back on.

"AAAAAAAAA-AAAAA-AAAAAH!"

DINKIN, MEET DANGER

Dinkins: 1
Dangers: 1
Other names mentioned
(beginning with D): 7

30 Dinkin froze in terror as his bespectacled double burst into laughter!

"Ha! That was great! You should have seen the look on your face!" The reflection stepped forward, still chuckling. Much to Dinkin's horror, the mirror rippled like a pool of water as the reflection stepped *out of the mirror* and into the room! He stood face-to-face with Dinkin, an exact duplicate . . . except for a pair of glasses.

"D-d-double . . . ," muttered a trembling Dinkin.

"You know, I often wondered whether my mirror was a doorway to another dimension," said Dinkin's living reflection, glancing back at the mirror. "Then all of a sudden, I'm looking in the mirror and what do I see? Your face staring back at me! An exact double! Except for my stylish eyewear, of course. I guess all it took was for us both to look in the mirror at exactly the same time, and the doorway between our dimensions opened."

"D-double . . . d-dimension . . . ," stuttered Dinkin, paralyzed with fear.

"What's wrong with you? What are you so nervous about?" said the double. But by now, Dinkin was much too terrified to speak. "The name's Danger," continued the double. "*Danger Duncan Dings*. What's yours?"

"D-D-D-," began Dinkin.

"Wait, let me guess—Dean? Daniel? Darren? Derrick? Drummond? Dorian?" asked Danger.

"D-Dinkin," w h i m p e r e d Dinkin.

"Dinkin? That's not even a real name," said Danger. "Well, *Dinkin*, I don't have time to stand around waiting for you to stop squeaking like a mouse—there are daring deeds that need to be done! Now, point me in the direction of something death defying before I die of boredom!"

"D-d-death defying?" said Dinkin as Danger sauntered over to the window and looked out. "No, wait, you can't! You have to go back! Don't you see? When we looked at each other's reflections, it activated the portal between your dimension and mine! The doorway is open! Who knows what other horrors might escape from Dimension 9!"

"An open door to my dimension? No, we definitely can't have that," said Danger, checking his watch.  He grabbed Dinkin's bathrobe from the back of the chair and threw it over the mirror. "There! That should stop anything else from coming through for now . . . "

"M-my bathrobe? Are you sure that will be enough to—," began Dinkin, but Danger's mind was already on other things.

"Hey, is that a *bike* on your porch?" he squealed, staring out the window.

"Y-yeah," muttered Dinkin. "My mom and dad bought it for my birthday."

"Why didn't you mention this fifty-six seconds ago? It looks brand-new!" cried Danger. "I mangled mine the day I got it riding off the roof . . . "

"You *rode it off the roof*?" squealed Dinkin—and then it hit him. Danger was a mirror image of him, *reversed* in every way! He wasn't scared of anything! Dinkin was 1.6 seconds through panicking about a fearless version of himself on the loose, when Danger raced out of the bedroom.

"W-wait! Come back! You have to go back in the mirror!" cried Dinkin, but Danger was already halfway downstairs. This was disastrous! Why did his mirror have to turn into a dimensional portal, today of all days? And how was he going to persuade his duplicate to go back through? Dinkin hurried

to the top of the stairs and peered over the banister as Danger strode into the kitchen and came face-to-face with Dinkin's parents.

"Are you all right, Dinkin? You look different somehow," said Mrs. Dings.

"He's decided to give the Hidden Danger Detection Glasses another try, of course! Good for you, Dink," said Mr. Dings.

"Dinkin's upstairs. I'm Danger," said Danger. "Pleased to meet you, alternative dimension Mom and Dad."

"Just once, I'd like to have a normal day," muttered Mrs. Dings, assuming this was just more of Dinkin's "silliness."

"Can I borrow Dinkin's bike? Can I, please?" said Danger.

"What about your soda?" asked Mrs. Dings. "It's nice and flat, just the way you like it."

"Flat soda? Yuck! I'd rather drink from the toilet! Which I would, if you dared me," said Danger.

"Ha! Those glasses are definitely still working," laughed Mr. Dings. "Yesterday you were *terrified* of that bike . . ."

"Terrified? I'm not terrified of anything!" said Danger. "I'm Danger Dings. Danger by name, daring by nature."

And with that, he ran out of the house and leaped onto the bike. Upstairs, Dinkin heard his mom shout, "Dinkin! Be careful!" He dashed to the window to see Danger speeding down the road.

"Oh no! He took the bike!" said Dinkin, tugging his hair. After another thirty-two seconds of panicking, he rushed downstairs to find his parents.

"Back so soon?" said Mr. Dings as Dinkin ran into the kitchen. "You only just left."

"That wasn't me, that was Danger!" cried Dinkin. "I was right all along—my reflection wasn't my reflection at all . . . he's a duplicate Dinkin named Danger! He came out of the mirror and now he's on the loose! We have to get him to go back and then close the doorway to Dimension 9!"

"Why don't we discuss it over some cookies? They've been soaking in water for twenty minutes . . . ," said Mrs. Dings, trying to be patient.

Dinkin hopped nervously from foot to foot. It was obvious his parents simply couldn't tell the difference between him and his other-dimensional duplicate. But he couldn't get Danger back into the mirror without help.

THiS WAS A JOB FOR THE FRiGHTENiNG THiNGS!

THE DANGER DILEMMA

Number of burps: 1
Number of The Frightening Things
eaten: 2
Number of times someone says
"AAAAH!": 6

Dinkin spent the rest of the evening trying
to convince his parents to help him look
for Danger, but it soon became obvious
they didn't even think his double was
real. In the end, Dinkin gave up and waited
until midnight. His parents had been in
bed for more than an hour when
Dinkin took the Ancient Summoning
Parchment from under the Ancient
Summoning Mattress, assumed the Ancient
Summoning Position, and spoke the Ancient
Summoning Chant:

"Frightening Things, Frightening Things
Creep from the gloom,
Crawl from the shadows and into my room,
Frightening Things, Frightening Things
Come to my aid,
Save me from danger (and being afraid!)."

Four-and-a-half seconds later, Dinkin heard a familiar growl from under his bed, and Herbert the monster crawled out. The scaly, green creature dragged himself sleepily to his feet and stretched his claws and tail.

"Where are the others, Herbert?" asked Dinkin. "This is an emergency!"

Herbert looked around, a little confused, and then held his belly. There was a low, rumbling sound, like a volcano about to erupt, and then . . .

Herbert let out an enormous belch, and Edgar and Arthur shot out of his mouth!

JUUURRKKRPP!

"AAAAAH!" screamed Dinkin as Edgar crashed to the floor, sending his head flying underneath Dinkin's dresser. Arthur the ghost was catapulted through the outside wall, only to reappear 1.6 seconds later.

"Eww!" he squealed, spinning around. "I've been *eaten*! Herbert, you . . . you . . . monster!"

"What's going on?" said Dinkin, retrieving Edgar's head and reattaching it to his body.

"That pea-brained beast ate us!" cried Edgar's head. "Swallowed us whole while we weren't looking!"

"Sorry about that," said Herbert, yawning and exposing a mouth full of sharp, yellow teeth. "I must have been sleep-eating again."

"Sleep-eating?" repeated Dinkin.

"That scale-bellied, greedy guts can't even stop eating when he's unconscious," moaned Edgar. "I'm pretty sure there's a lampshade and two pairs of socks in that bottomless pit he calls a stomach."

"I can't help it," said Herbert. "Eating

and sleeping are my main priorities. After panicking, that is."

"I can't tell what's ectoplasm and what's monster slobber!" cried Arthur, trying to wring Herbert's saliva out of his rear end. "Honestly, the amount of drool he generates is nothing short of terrifying."

"Well, I bet it's not as terrifying as Danger Dings, the double from Dimension 9!" cried Dinkin.

"AAAA-AA-AH!" screamed The Frightening Things.

"N-not Dimension 9!" wailed Arthur. "Um, which one's Dimension 9?"

"Do you know, I'm not quite sure . . . is it the time-goes-backward dimension?" replied Edgar.

"No, no, no, that's Dimension 15! Honestly, am I the only one who knows about Dimension 9?" said Dinkin, and he grabbed a large, thick notebook from his shelf. On its cover were the words:

"AAAAAAAAAAH! Not Volume Two!"
screamed The Frightening Things together.

Dinkin's *Secret History of the Terrifying*
covered almost every aspect of his terrors,
dilemmas, fears, and phobias. Dinkin
nervously opened the book to the first page.

44

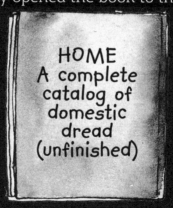

He turned to the contents page.

Dinkin skipped to chapter five and read aloud:

CHECK YOUR REFLECTION!

If you notice anything even slightly different about the way you look, it is 98.4% likely that you are NOT looking at your reflection, but at a doom-bringing DOUBLE FROM DIMENSION 9—the same-but-different dimension! Run!*

*NOTE: If running away isn't a realistic
long-term option, the only way to
close the dimensional door is to send
everything from Dimension 9
back into the mirror!

"AAAAAH!" screamed The Frightening Things again.

"Exactly!" said Dinkin. "But wait, there's more . . . "

One hour and twenty-nine minutes later (there was quite a lot more screaming), Dinkin had explained all about his Danger dilemma—about the glasses, the mirror, and the terrifyingly fearless (and currently missing) Dinkin duplicate.

"So, he's really not afraid of *anything*?" said Herbert.

"No! And he's been gone all night! On my bike! Who knows if he's even still alive! He could be in a ditch somewhere with the bike chain wrapped around his neck . . . which means we'll never get him back in the mirror! And every second he's here is another second the dimensional doorway is left open!"

That moment, a small stone bounced off Dinkin's bedroom window.

"AAAAH!" screamed The Frightening Things. "Meteor shower!"

Dinkin and The Frightening Things searched for somewhere to take cover, but after two more stones had hit the window, Dinkin made a desperate dash for his bed to retrieve his comet-slowing De-meteorizer (a whisk with three bendy straws wrapped around it) from under his pillow. He crept nervously up to the window and peered out.

47

There, on the front lawn, was Danger Dings, throwing dirt from the driveway up at the window. Dinkin was so relieved to see his bespectacled double that he opened the window and stuck his head out.

"Danger! Where have you been?" cried Dinkin.

"Where *haven't* I been?" laughed Danger. He shimmied up the drainpipe as if he was climbing a ladder, scrambled onto the windowsill and swung effortlessly into Dinkin's room. He was soaking wet and covered in leaves, dirt, cuts, and bruises.

"What happened? Are you all right? You've been gone for ages! Did my bike attack you?" asked Dinkin.

"Your bike? I smashed that up hours ago trying to jump over a trailer. And then I dodged traffic on the freeway, chased after a herd of cows, and took a swim in the local reservoir. Oh, and then I found a spider and

let it crawl all over my hand! What a night!"
said Danger, taking off his damp socks and
wringing them out.

"A spider? Wow, he really *is* brave . . . ,"
said Herbert. Danger spun round. The
Frightening Things were huddled in a corner.
They smiled nervously and each gave a little
wave.

"AAAAH!" screamed Danger, louder than
anyone had screamed all night! "Get them
away from me! Save me, Dinkin! Save me!"

"Okay, maybe he's not *that* brave," said
Herbert.

HOW TO DEAL WITH DANGER

Actual time: 02:10 AM
"Dinkin" time: ten past terror

50 The Frightening Things stared in disbelief as Dinkin's so-called fearless double shrieked in terror and tried to climb back out of the window!

"AAAA-AAH! *They're after me*! HELP!" screamed Danger.

"Wait! Danger, it's all right! I summoned them. They're my *friends*!" cried Dinkin.

"Don't let them get me! Somebody, please help!" squealed Danger, already halfway out of the window. "W-wait a minute, did you say *friends*?"

"Yeah! This is Herbert, Edgar, and Arthur—The Frightening Things. I summoned them here," said Dinkin. Danger clambered slowly back into the room. He saw that the mirror was still covered and breathed a small sigh of relief. He edged cautiously toward The Frightening Things and inspected them carefully.

"Hey, you're not . . . You're not frightening at all!" he said in amazement.

"Well excuu-use us," said Edgar. "You try being frightening after spending half the night in a monster's mouth . . . "

51

"Ha! Sorry . . . for a moment I thought you were someone else," said Danger. He gave Herbert a poke in the belly and wafted his hand through Arthur's face. "But you're not, are you? You're not them!"

"Them? Them who?" asked Dinkin. "What were you so afraid of?"

"Afraid? Who's afraid? I'm not afraid of anything!" replied Danger, leaping onto the bed and bouncing off into the air. He landed on Herbert's shoulders and began riding him around the room. "I'm Danger Dings! Danger by name, daring by nature!"

Danger spent the rest of the night entertaining everyone with stories of his courageous feats. Dinkin tried his best to persuade Danger to go back to Dimension 9, but Danger was having way too much fun in this dimension to even consider it. The Frightening Things, too, seemed to forget the horror of having an open dimensional door in the bedroom. In fact, they all seemed extremely impressed by Danger's tales of fear-flouting fun.

"No way! So you really once jumped off the roof of your house into a swimming pool?" asked Herbert.

"And you really climbed onto the top of a telephone pole wearing nothing but a bathing suit?" added Edgar.

"And you really rode Dinkin's bike? With no hands or anything?" asked Arthur.

"All true!" laughed Danger. "Hey, that's me—Danger by name . . . "

"Daring by nature!" said The Frightening Things gleefully, but a moment later, they began to fade. Dinkin stared out the window as the sun began to rise over the rooftops.

"That's it for another night—sorry, Dinkin. Stay safe . . . Oh, and terrifying to meet you, Danger," said Edgar, and with that, The Frightening Things disappeared, leaving Dinkin alone with his disturbingly devil-may-care dimensional duplicate.

"Well, I suppose you'll be wanting to go back where you came from, too," began Dinkin hopefully. "Back to your own dimension . . . "

"You're not still going on about that, are you?" said Danger. "I'm not going anywhere—I like it much better here. If you're so concerned, why don't *you* go through the mirror?"

"WHAT? No way! Who knows what new terrors might await me in Dimension 9! My life's scary enough as it is! I've got to get through breakfast, brushing my teeth, getting dressed—not to mention a whole day of school!"

"You're scared of *school*?" asked Danger.

"Of course! School is terrifying!" replied Dinkin. "It's the eleventh most terrifying place in the world, just after shark cages and petting zoos! And with all this Dimension 9 business, I haven't even had time to reinforce my Playground Protection Pants or charge the Emergency Lunch Launcher 2.1 or mix up a new batch of Bully-B-Gone repellent spray! I'm doomed!"

"School isn't terrifying!" said Danger. "And it's definitely better than being stuck at home all day. At least there's a slim chance you might get to do *something* daring."

Dinkin couldn't believe what he was hearing! How could Danger, or anyone, actually *want* to go to school? Then (3.8 seconds later), an idea occurred to him. It was such a brilliantly, fear-avoidingly phenomenal idea that Dinkin had to try hard not to clap his hands together with excitement.

"You know, you could go to school for me," he said, trying to sound casual. "I mean, if you think you can handle all the terrifyingness."

"What? Of course I could! I can handle anything! But are you sure you don't mind?" said Danger, his bespectacled eyes lighting up.

"Anything for my other-dimensional twin," said Dinkin with a grin. "But do me a favor, if anyone calls you Dinkin, just pretend to be me, will you? It'll, uh, make it more daring!"

Danger grinned a wide, thrill-seeking grin. "You've got yourself a deal, Dinkin Dings."

One minute and eleven seconds later, Danger was dressed in Dinkin's school uniform. Except for his glasses, it was impossible to tell them apart.

"So what are you going to do while I'm being you?" asked Danger as he straightened his tie.

"I'm going to do what I always do," replied Dinkin. "Hide and panic."

A moment later, the door swung open. Dinkin dived behind it as his mother poked her head into the room and came face- to-face with Danger.

"Oh good, you're up," began Dinkin's mom. "And dressed for school already! What a good boy!

57

Oh, Dinkin, I like this new you!"

"What do you mean, *new* me?" said Danger. "I'm not a new me. I'm the old me! I'm Dinkin! Dinkin Dings, from this dimension! Now, what's for breakfast?" he said, ushering Dinkin's mom out of the room. Dinkin breathed a sigh of relief and slumped to the floor. He stayed in his room, waiting for his plan to fall apart. But at 8:22 he heard the bus pull up outside his house and crept to the window. Sure enough, Danger raced out of the house and bounded fearlessly on board. Dinkin laughed in joyful disbelief! He'd gotten out of going to school!

And he hadn't even needed to chain himself to the bed!

THE PERFECT PLAN

Time spent on inventions: 2 hours,
2 minutes
Time spent worrying: 1 hour, 6
minutes
Time before The Perfect Plan
turns out to be less than perfect: 3
hours, 17 minutes

Dinkin couldn't believe it—a day off from
school. It was The Perfect Plan! Maybe Danger
would have such a good time that he'd want
to go everyday! Dinkin would *never* have to
face school ever again. The possibility made
the idea of an open doorway to Dimension 9
in his bedroom a lot more bearable. Dinkin
waited quietly for his mom and dad to go to
work so that he could leave his room, but
by then he was too nervous to go anywhere
in an empty house full of who-knows-what
hidden horrors. It was one hour and six

minutes later when he finally got up the courage to collect everything he needed for a day's inventing. Before long, Dinkin was in his stride. By lunchtime he had:

1) Mixed up a fresh batch of Bully-B-Gone spray (made up of equal parts rotten eggs, vinegar, toilet water, liquid soap, furniture polish, Tabasco sauce, and his mom's least favorite perfume, all mixed up together in his mom's least favorite perfume bottle)

2) Re-tuned the television so that it didn't pick up any channels, reducing the risk of mind control by 37.65%

3) Drawn up blueprints for his all-new, all-indestructible Fortress of Absolute, Total, and Utter Protection (this time with extra-thick cardboard)

Not only that, but he recorded forty-six existing fears and discovered sixty-one new terrors. He was halfway through listing the top ten most terrifying sandwich fillings when he heard the front door open.

"Dinkin? Dinkin?" came the cry. It was his mother. Dinkin scrambled to his feet and looked for a place to hide. He'd almost squeezed himself into the cabinet under the sink when his mother spotted him.

"What are you doing back home?" she cried, dragging him out by his pajamas. "I've been worried sick about you! The school called to say you'd run away!"

"What? I mean, no! I mean, yes, but . . . I thought I was at school!" said Dinkin, panicking on at least three levels. *Why wasn't Danger still at school? Where had he gone?*

"Dinkin, I've told you a hundred times: You can't just run away from school whenever you feel like it! I had to leave Mrs. Oldengray to look after the shop, and you know how useless she is—she'll have probably burned the whole place down by now!" said Mrs. Dings. Dinkin pictured Mrs. Oldengray (who smelled like dust and was so ancient that Dinkin was sure she was mostly ghostly) standing in the middle of his mom's flower shop, laughing manically with a lit match in her hand. He had just started to panic about it when his mother interrupted. "Well, you're going straight back! Where's your uniform? Put it on this instant!"

"My . . . my uniform?" whimpered Dinkin, looking down at his pajamas. He couldn't tell his mom that his dimensional double was wearing his uniform—and had gone to school—in his place. She'd never believe him! He had to come up with something that didn't sound too farfetched or ridiculous. Finally, he said, "It was eaten!"

"Eaten?"

"Eaten! Nibbled to nothingness by mutant moths from the moon!" said Dinkin.

"Well, it's a good thing I bought you a spare set then, isn't it?" growled Mrs. Dings, marching Dinkin to her bedroom. She reached into her closet and pulled out a brand-new school uniform. Dinkin's mother had gotten into the habit of buying two of everything as Dinkin often became convinced that certain items of clothing were "out to get him."

"Now put these on—*you are going back to school*. I want you ready in five minutes."

Four minutes and fifty-eight seconds later, Dinkin was in his mom's car, complete with his spare school bag slung over his shoulder. As they pulled up outside the school, Dinkin was kicking himself for trusting Danger.

"And I don't want to get another call from the school," said Mrs. Dings, ushering Dinkin out of the car. "Do I make myself clear?"

"Yes, Mom," said Dinkin as Mrs. Dings led him into school and down the hall to his classroom. All of 5D giggled at the sight of Dinkin being steered to his desk by his mother.

"Dinkin Dings, how nice of you to rejoin us," said Ms. Feebleback, clearly not happy to see him.

"Sorry about this," said Mrs. Dings. "I made Dinkin promise he'd sit tight for the rest of the day."

"Let's hope so. I don't know what got into him earlier . . . ," said Ms. Feebleback. "And you might want to stop by the principal on your way out—he's not too happy about the fire department having to come."

"The *fire department*?" said Dinkin and Mrs. Dings together. Mrs. Dings put her head in her hands, then shot Dinkin an incredibly stern look through her fingers.

"We'll talk about this at home," she said through gritted teeth, and left.

"Hey, Dinkin! What happened to your funny glasses?" asked Misty Spittle, spraying Dinkin with saliva.

"Duh, they're probably still on the roof!" said Talbot Toploft.

"The roof? What roof?" squeaked Dinkin in terror.

"Duh, the school roof! Don't you remember?" said Talbot Toploft.

"Wait, he was—I mean, *I* was on the school roof?" whispered Dinkin, fear gripping him. "I mean, of course I remember . . . but just remind me—what was I doing on the school roof?"

"Cartwheels, mostly," sprayed Misty Spittle. "And then you tried pole vaulting off the roof into a tree with a TV antenna. It was pretty exciting actually, especially when the fire department showed up to get you down . . ."

The fire department?! thought Dinkin, rocking back and forth in unbridled terror. How could he have been so stupid as to trust Danger? All he'd done was get Dinkin in trouble! Even worse, he had no idea where Danger was now, or what daring deeds he was doing in Dinkin's name! He had to find him, but there was no way Ms. Feebleback would let him out of her sight now. He was debating whether to try crawling under the desks when a ball of scrunched-up paper hit him in the head. He looked around to see Boris Wack (the biggest boy in class 5D) staring at him with an angry look on his face and clenching his enormous fists. Dinkin picked up the piece of paper and opened it.

On it was written:

SEA YOU IN THE PLAYGROWND (YOUR DEAD)

"AAH!" screamed Dinkin as quietly as he could. A death threat! And a badly spelled one at that! He looked again, and noticed something on the other side of the paper. Shaking with fear, he turned it over.

Dear Boris,
Who are you calling "Four-Eyes"?
Meet me in the playground after school.
It's time to find out who's the toughest kid in 5D! Or are you too much of a thumb-sucking girly-wirly to face me?
Yours sincerely,
~~Danger~~ DiNKiN Dings

"AAAAAAH!" screamed Dinkin, much more loudly than before. Danger had challenged Boris Wack to a fight!

"Dinkin Dings!" screeched Ms. Feebleback. "I have officially run out of patience with you! I don't want to hear another peep out of you for the rest of the day! Is that clear?"

"But—," began Dinkin.

"Not a peep!"

Dinkin put his hand over his mouth and sat in terrified silence as he felt Boris's vengeful stare burning into the back of his head. Finally, he checked his watch.

2:04.

He had one hour and twenty-six minutes to live.

BULLY-B-GONE

Ingredients in one bottle of
Bully-B-Gone: 7
Amount of Bully-B-Gone used to
repel Boris Wack: 1/2 a bottle
Amount of times Dinkin is called
"Stinkin' Dings": 113

70 One hour and twenty-two minutes of hopeless panicking later, Dinkin suddenly remembered something *incredibly* important—he'd packed the new bottle of Bully-B-Gone repellent in his bag! He took it out and held it tightly under the desk. Then, with only minutes to go before the bell, he began spraying himself all over. By the time he'd emptied half the bottle on his clothes, everyone in the classroom was holding their nose. Even Roddy Jollify, who had tissues stuffed up his nostrils to stop his nosebleeds, began to feel faint from the smell.

"Ms. Feebleback! Dinkin's stinky!" cried Misty Spittle, flaring her vast, black-hole nostrils.

"Duh! He's 'Stinkin' Dings'!" laughed Talbot Toploft. Four point four seconds later, the whole class was chanting:

"STINKIN' DINGS, STINKIN' DINGS, HE'S THE BOY WHO SMELLS OF THINGS!"

"What's all this racket? Oh my!" cried Ms. Feebleback, almost fainting as the cloud of Bully-B-Gone reached her. "What *is* that? It smells like . . . like the end of the world!"

Dinkin watched in relief as the entire class began moving their desks to get away from him. Some were even climbing over one another to try and get away—especially

Boris Wack, who, as a fully qualified bully, was more affected by the spray than anyone. He started squealing and flapping his arms, knocking over two chairs and four children in his attempts to escape the stench. Dinkin couldn't help but smile at the sight, even though he had doomed himself to the nickname "Stinkin' Dings" for all eternity.

"Dinkin Dings, this is the last straw! Get out of my classroom this very minute!" shouted Ms. Feebleback.

"Are . . . are you sure, Ms. Feebleback? The bell hasn't rung yet," said Dinkin nervously.

"Out!" screeched Ms. Feebleback.

Dinkin ran out of the classroom with the "Stinkin' Dings!" chant ringing in his ears, and didn't stop running until he was home. He found the key under the mat, opened the door, and closed it behind him. He was safe . . . at least until tomorrow. He was about to make his way into the kitchen when he heard the sound of talking. It was his parents—and *Danger*. They'd found him! Dinkin tiptoed upstairs and peered over the banister again as Danger followed his parents out of the kitchen and into the hall.

"We're very disappointed in you, Dinkin," said Mr. Dings. "Not only because you climbed onto the school roof, and you tried to pole vault with the TV antenna, and the fire department had to get you down."

"But *then*," said Mrs. Dings, shaking with rage, "less than three hours after I find you at home, after I take you all the way back to school, after you *promise* you'll behave yourself—I get a call from Mrs. Oldengray in the flower shop to say that she's seen you riding down the street on the back of a garbage truck!"

"Yeah, that was *especially* brave," chortled Danger.

"How on earth did you get out of school? And how did you get into town so quickly? And what . . . and how . . . and *why* . . . ?" said Mrs. Dings, too enraged to form actual sentences.

"I think what your mother is *trying* to say, Dink," sighed Mr. Dings, "is that this is just not acceptable behavior . . . even for you. We're supposed to be at work—we can't spend all day chasing after you! Honestly, ever since we gave you those glasses, you've been acting even stranger than usual . . . "

"Oh, so you'd rather I was a complete chicken, like Dinkin?" said Danger.

"What do you mean, 'like Dinkin'?" replied Mr. Dings.

"I mean, like me!" said Danger quickly.

"Oh, I've had enough! Go to your room this instant. We'll talk about this over dinner," said Mrs. Dings.

Danger shrugged and began trudging up the stairs. Dinkin hurried back to his bedroom in case his parents were following. But as he looked for a hiding place, he noticed something unsettlingly different about his room. He clamped his hand over his mouth and stifled a scream.

His mirror was missing.

Where had it gone? It was the only way to send Danger home!

"You *stink*, Dinkin," said a voice. Dinkin spun around in terror to see Danger in the doorway. "What's that rotten smell?"

"Nevermind that, it's just Bully-B-Gone!" said Dinkin in his most terrified (and enraged) whisper. "Where's the mirror? What have you done with it?"

"I haven't done anything with it! Um, I mean, what mirror?" replied Danger, trying to sound innocent.

"My mirror! The doorway to Dimension 9! The only way to send you back to where you came from! It was right there, and now it's gone!" cried Dinkin.

"I don't know . . . I guess it must have been stolen by . . . mirror thieves," said Danger, scratching his head.

"Mirror thieves?" said Dinkin, nervous and a little suspicious.

"Yeah, or something like that," said Danger with a shrug. "Anyway, it looks like I'm stuck here forever!"

"What? No, you can't stay!" said Dinkin. "You've only been here a day and I'm already in more trouble than I've been in all year!

We have to find that mirror. We have to send you back to Dimension 9!"

"You worry too much, Dinkin," Danger said. "This is best for both of us! You get to hide all day in your room, and I get to be extra-daring 'cause everyone thinks I'm a scaredy-cat. You'll see, life is so much better when I'm you!"

"But—you can't be me! *I'm* me! I was here first!" cried Dinkin.

"Yeah, well, you're never going to find that mirror, so there's nothing you can do about it," said Danger smugly.

"What do you mean, I'll never find it? Do you . . . do you know where it is? Be honest!" asked Dinkin.

"Of course not!" said Danger quickly.

"I wonder what's for dinner—I'm starving! You stay here—if you're lucky, I'll bring you some leftovers!"

And with that, Danger raced downstairs. Dinkin sat down on his bed and held his stomach as it rumbled with hunger. Three things were suddenly clear:

1. This dimension wasn't big enough for the two of them.

2. The mirror hadn't been stolen by "mirror thieves." Danger had hidden it.

3. He wasn't going to get any dinner.

Dinkin only had one choice: He had to find that mirror and send Danger back.

This was a job for The Frightening Things.

A JOB FOR THE FRIGHTENING THINGS

Risk of waking the duplicate:
6,599 scariness pounds
Time spent looking for Dinkin's
mirror: 3 hours, 43 minutes
Sheds: 1

Dinkin changed out of his smelly clothes, threw them into his closet, and put on a recently disinfected pair of pajamas. He waited nervously and hungrily in his room as Danger ate his dinner (7:01), tried to watch a show about extreme sports on the broken television (7:45), and attempted to juggle with a carving knife and a barbecue fork (8:27) before Mr. Dings stopped him. Finally (9:23), Danger made his way to bed. Dinkin hid underneath the bed as his mom tucked Danger in.

"We can both see that you're different, Dinkin," said Mrs. Dings as she pulled the covers around Danger's chin. "And it's not that we're not happy to see you being a little more . . . bold, but try not to get into any trouble for a while, okay?"

"I'll try," said Danger.

"And don't stay up all night talking to those 'Frightening Things' of yours," added Mrs. Dings, kissing Danger on the head.

"You don't have to worry about The Frightening Things,"

said Danger. "They won't be bothering me anymore. In fact, this is going to be the best night's sleep I've had in a long time."

Dinkin waited for his mom to leave and then crawled out from under the bed.

"What did you mean about The Frightening Things not bothering you?" he asked as Danger rolled over and closed his eyes.

"It doesn't matter," said Danger with a yawn. "Let's just say it's probably a good thing your mirror's . . . gone."

Hidden, you mean . . . by you! thought Dinkin. He huddled in the corner of the room, listening to the sound of Danger's snoring. Then, as the clock struck midnight, he stopped huddling and took the Ancient Summoning Parchment out of his pajama pocket. He assumed the Ancient Summoning Position and whispered his quietest Ancient Summoning Chant:

"Frightening Things, Frightening Things
Creep from the gloom,

Crawl from the shadows and into my room,
Frightening Things, Frightening Things
Come to my aid,
Save me from danger (and being afraid!)."

Edgar the skeleton was the first to appear.

He stumbled out of the closet, waving his arms and screaming.

"AAH! That smell! It smells like the end of the world!"

"*Shhhhh*! Don't wake the double!" whispered Dinkin, snapping Edgar's jaw shut.

"It's just my clothes . . . and a little Bully-B-Gone spray . . ."

A moment later, the window swung open and Arthur the ghost swept into the room. "It's freezing out there! Honestly, if I'd known how cold the afterlife was, I never would have stuck around . . . ," he moaned.

"*SShhH!!* Don't wake the double!"

whispered Dinkin, pointing to the bed. Suddenly, the air was filled with an almighty *BUUUURRP!* and Herbert the monster crawled out from under the bed.

"*SHHH-HH!* Don't wake the—never mind," said Dinkin as Danger's snoring filled the room. "Just follow me!"

Dinkin ushered The Frightening Things out onto the landing. After a quick explanation of the terrifying events of the day, Dinkin spelled out the plan.

"So you see, the only solution is to get Danger back to his own dimension. We have to find out where he's hidden my mirror!"

Dinkin and The Frightening Things decided it was best to split up to look for the mirror . . . but then they immediately realized that was much too terrifying, so they searched as a team. Three hours and thirty-three minutes later, they had scoured the entire house, even the incredibly scary bits, including:

1) The downstairs toilet (32% risk of alligator attack)

2) The bit of discolored carpet by the back door (54% risk of stain-festation)

3) The garage (77% risk of catching a nasty chill, even in the height of summer)

But there was no sign of the mirror. The only place they hadn't dared to check was the attic, which they had sworn never to go in after all that "creature from the attic" business. Dinkin and The Frightening Things stood beneath the hatch, staring upward.

"Arthur, couldn't you just take a peek up there?" said  Dinkin, shivering with fear and exhaustion. "I mean, you are a ghost— it's not like anything can hurt you . . ."

"No way! I'm not going into the attic!" said Arthur. "I'd rather go to the middle of a volcano! I'd rather go to the lost land of less than lovable lizard-ladies! I'd rather . . . I'd rather go into the garden shed!"

"The garden shed?" repeated Dinkin. "That's it! The one place we haven't looked!"

"*AAAAH!* Not the shed!" cried Arthur. "I'd rather go into the attic!"

Dinkin steered The (reluctant) Frightening

Things downstairs and into the kitchen. After unlocking the fifteen locks on the back door, they stepped cautiously outside and stared into the moonlit garden. Everything that used to be just terrifying (trees, flowers, fish pond) now looked hideously horrifying. And there, lurking in the shadows, was THE SHED.

Dinkin had always been afraid of the shed, for three very good reasons:

1) It was crawling with SPIDERS. Spiders, as anyone who has ever been scared will tell you, were the First of All Scary Things. Before tornadoes and volcanoes and dinosaurs, before tidal waves and comets and mutant centipedes and man-eating vegetables, there were SPIDERS.

2) It was where Dinkin's dad kept his disturbingly large collection of SEEDS. Though they were marked with names like "Freesias" and "Sweet Peas" and "Nasturtiums," Dinkin knew what the seeds really were: an Easy-2-Grow Army of Unspeakable Plant People!

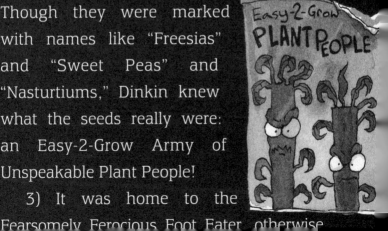

3) It was home to the Fearsomely Ferocious Foot Eater, otherwise

known as THE LAWNMOWER. Not only did it cut grass, trim borders, and eat feet, but it made such an earsplitting noise that Dinkin was convinced that it caused earthquakes on neighboring streets.

But these were terrors for another time. They had to search the shed, no matter what.

"You know, considering how scared we are of everything, we do spend an awful lot of time doing scary things," said Edgar, his bones rattling with dread. "Couldn't we just hide in the closet until all of this goes away?"

"I like that plan!" said Herbert.

"Me too!" said Arthur, with excitement.

"But Danger's not going to go away!" said Dinkin. "In fact, unless we find that mirror and send him back, he's going to stay here forever! Is that what you want? Do you want to be stuck with a duplicate version of me, whose idea of a good time is picking fights with the biggest boy in school?" Dinkin didn't wait for an answer. He set off down the garden, closely followed by The Frightening Things. They crept across the lawn, their eyes darting around for any signs of unexpected scariness.

"D-don't stop moving," whispered Dinkin. "And no screaming, unless absolutely necessary."

"What, not even a ghostly moan?" asked Arthur.

"Okay, b-but keep it quiet," said Dinkin.

Arthur moaned his quietest, fear-filled moan as they made their way to the shed. It loomed over them: They could almost smell the horrors lurking inside. Dinkin reached out a shaking hand toward the door and turned the handle. It clicked and clunked ominously, and then gave way.

"Shhhh!" said Dinkin instinctively, and poked his head around the door. The moonlight seeped in through the wooden planks of the walls, bathing everything in

a menacing glow. The shed was arranged with an unsettling neatness, probably to set a good example for the Unspeakable Plant People. Dinkin and The Frightening Things crept in, their eyes peeled for spiders and seeds. They did their best to look around, but everyone was so afraid of moving or touching anything that they mainly just stood in one place and shivered with fear.

Suddenly, Dinkin spotted something propped up in the corner. It was a large, rectangular shape . . . *covered by a bathrobe*.

"I see it!" whispered Dinkin.

"See what? I can hardly see a thing in this darkness," mumbled Herbert. "Except that big spider web, of course . . . "

"Did you say . . . spider web?" whispered Dinkin. There was a pause.

AAAA-AAHH!" screamed Dinkin and The Frightening Things together. "SPIDERS!"

The prospect of coming face to legs with a spider was simply too terrifying to bear. Arthur started whizzing around the shed like a spinning top, while Edgar shook so hard his leg fell off. Herbert collided into Dinkin, who stumbled back into the door, pushing it open. He fell onto the cold ground and looked up. A face very much like his peered down at him.

"Looking for something, Dinkin?"

It was Danger!

DANGER'S SECRET

Mirrors located: 1
Sinister secrets revealed: 1
Chance of everything turning
out fine and there being
nothing at all to worry about:
0.000000000000001%

94   Dinkin scrambled to his feet and slammed
the shed door shut, leaving The Frightening
Things still inside.

"We weren't looking for anything,
honest!" he blurted quickly.

"You mean you didn't find . . . I mean,
you weren't looking for . . . ," began Danger.

"Nope! And we definitely didn't find it,
either!" cried Dinkin.

"Dinkin, we found it! We found the
mirror!" cried Arthur, poking his head
through the shed wall.

"The mirror? Oh no! Whatever you do, don't uncover it!" yelled Danger. He pushed Dinkin out of the way and burst into the shed! There were Arthur, Edgar, and Herbert, huddled around Dinkin's mirror. Herbert had Dinkin's bathrobe in his claws.

"Cover it back up! It's after midnight!" cried Danger.

"Why? What happens after midnight?" asked Dinkin.

Suddenly, the mirror began to shake and rattle, sending tremors through the ground, and steam began to pour out of the glass!

"It's The Frightening Things!" cried Danger. "RUN!"

"The who?" said Dinkin as Danger shoved him aside again and started to run back up the garden. As confused as Dinkin and The Frightening Things were, they didn't wait around for an explanation—they ran out of the shed after Danger, slamming the door behind them. They were almost at the house when Dinkin looked back . . .

CRAS - SSH!

The door of the shed burst open! Dinkin stared in horror as three huge, nonhuman shapes emerged from inside. He could barely make them out, but it was already clear what they were. The first was a huge skeleton with fire smoldering in its skull, illuminating its eye sockets from inside. Next came a ghoulish spirit, like an angry cloud of greenish-white smoke, which swept into the air. Finally there was a giant monster, almost big enough to fill the entire shed! Its body was covered in horns and spikes, which glistened with slime in the moonlight. It gnashed its huge, fang-filled jaws in rage.

"DANGER . . . WE'RE COMING FOR YOU," hissed the skeleton.

Dinkin froze in horror. Suddenly, it all made a terrifying kind of sense.

They were The Frightening Things from Dimension 9!

And they were *actually* frightening!

ATTACK OF THE *ACTUALLY* FRIGHTENING THINGS

Skeletons: 2
Monsters: 2
Ghosts: 2

"Into the house!" yelled Dinkin as The *Actually* Frightening Things began moving up the garden. As soon as everyone was inside, Dinkin slammed the door and locked the locks.

"What in the name of all-that-is-horrendous *are* those things?" shrieked Edgar. "They're like . . . us! Sort of . . . "

"I know what they are—they're *Danger's* Frightening Things, aren't they, Danger?" said Dinkin. "That's why you didn't want to go back! You were scared!"

"No! I'm not scared of anything!" said Danger as he cowered behind the kitchen bin. "Well, except them . . . "

"I should have guessed! I knew something was up when you were scared of *my* Frightening Things. Why didn't you tell us about them before?" Dinkin asked.

"I didn't want you to think I was like you!" exclaimed Danger. "The Frightening Things are the only things I'm afraid of. They come after midnight, whether I like it or not. They play tricks on me, tie me up, steal my things, keep me awake — and scare me!"

BOOM!

The back door shook as something crashed against it. They could hear the monster's growls from the other side. Then came a *tap-tap-tap* at the kitchen window. Everyone looked up to see the face of the skeleton peering through.

"LET US IN, DANGER . . . IT'S WAY PAST YOUR FRIGHTENING TIME," it said, its eyes glowing in the darkness.

"G-go away!" cried Danger, but the ghost had already begun to seep through the door. As Dinkin, Danger, and The Frightening Things looked on, too terrified to even sniffle fearfully, a face emerged from the cloud of billowing smoke. Two hollow, black eyes peered at them, and a shadowy grin spread across its face. A moment later, the ghost

wrapped its tendrils around the locks, and undid them. The door swung open, and, within moments, Dinkin and his friends were face to fang with The *Actually* Frightening Things.

"WHO ARE YOUR FRIENDS, DANGER?" said the skeleton. "YOU KNOW WE DON'T LIKE YOU TO HAVE FRIENDS . . . "

"Th-they're d-dimensional d-doubles," whimpered Danger.

"ARE THEY? SO THEY ARE!" said the skeleton, pointing a sharp, bony finger at Dinkin. "WHY, THAT ONE LOOKS LIKE YOU! AND THERE'S A LITTLE GHOST, A SMALL SKELETON . . . EVEN A TINY MONSTER!"

103

"N-nice to m-m-meet you," said Herbert, always at his most polite when scared stiff. Suddenly the ghost blew a puff of greenish-white smoke in his face  and Herbert fell to the floor, fast asleep!

"SPEAK WHEN YOU'RE SPOKEN TO, OR YOU GET SENT TO SLEEP," laughed the skeleton. "AND WHILE WE'RE ON THE SUBJECT, GO AND MAKE SURE THE GROWN-UPS DON'T WAKE UP UNTIL MORNING." The ghost swept out of the room and up the stairs.

"M-mom! D-dad!" whispered Dinkin. He contemplated trying to warn them about the atrocious intruders, but then decided it was probably best if they just slept through it.

"NOW THEN, TIME FOR SOME FUN! WHAT SHALL WE PLAY?" hissed the skeleton. "OH, I KNOW! WHO WANTS TO PLAY 'WHO CAN SCREAM THE LOUDEST?'"

The monster roared, shaking the walls!

"NOT YOU, YOU IDIOT!" said the skeleton, covering his ear holes. "YOU DON'T GET TO PLAY THIS GAME. YOU ALWAYS GIVE ME A SKULL-ACHE WITH THAT HORRIBLE ROARING!"

As the skeleton gave the monster a scolding, Dinkin had just enough time to look for an escape route. The monster blocked the back door, while the skeleton barred the entrance to the hall. In desperation, Dinkin looked up and spotted Arthur hovering above his head in helpless horror. Slowly, he reached out and grabbed Edgar's bony wrist and then nodded to Edgar to grab hold of Danger's collar. Then, even though Danger was more scared than any of them, he managed

"SORRY ABOUT THAT—I'M AFRAID THE MONSTER CAN BE SO RUDE," said the skeleton. "SO, WHERE WERE WE? OH YES, SCREAMING! WHO WANTS TO START?"

Dinkin raised his arm. His hand was 1.4 inches away from Arthur's.

"WE HAVE A VOLUNTEER! EXCELLENT!"

Dinkin took a deep, terrified breath, and screamed: "ARTHUR, GRAB MY HAND!"

Arthur looked down at Dinkin's outstretched hand and instinctively grasped it, turning everyone ghostly. They could pass through anything! "Get us out of here!" yelled Dinkin. Arthur flew into the air, taking Dinkin, Edgar, Danger, and the unconscious Herbert with him. The monster roared in rage as they flew through the skeleton's ribcage and out into the hall.

"AFTER THEM!" hissed the skeleton.

"Arthur, fly us upstairs. We have to hide!" shouted Dinkin, possibly more terrified than he had ever been. Arthur flew the dread-filled daisy chain of unlikely allies up the stairs and onto the landing where they were met by the swirling, cloud-like ghost.

"AAAH!" screamed everyone, except the sleeping Herbert, as the ghost fired a blast of sleep-inducing breath. Arthur arched upward, flying everyone through the ceiling, and into the attic!

"AAA-AAH! THE ATTIC! Get us out of here!" screamed Dinkin. Arthur immediately flew back through the floor onto the landing, only to find the ghost waiting for them. It blew another cloud of breath into Arthur's face, and he immediately fell asleep, dropping Dinkin and company onto the landing. As Arthur drifted drowsily down the hallway, Dinkin scrambled to his feet.

into my room. Quick!" yelled Dinkin. He shoved Danger into his room and then turned back to help Edgar with Herbert.

"He's too heavy!" said Edgar as he and Dinkin tried to drag the sleeping monster along the ground. "I told him to lose weight! This is what happens when you eat in your sleep. You end up—"

Suddenly, two massive shadows loomed over them. Dinkin and Edgar looked up to see the skeleton and the monster blocking their paths.

". . . huge . . ." whimpered Dinkin.

"YOU'RE SLIPPERY LITTLE CREATURES, AREN'T YOU? BUT YOU CAN'T GET AWAY FROM US THAT EASILY! NOT WHEN THE GAMES HAVE ONLY JUST BEGUN!" sneered the skeleton, reaching down and scooping up Dinkin and Edgar in its bony claws.

"Please don't eat me!" pleaded Edgar. "I've had my fill of being ingested!"

"EAT YOU! WHAT AN EXCELLENT IDEA! THAT SHOULD GET THE FEAR FLOWING!"

The skeleton brought Dinkin and Edgar closer to his flame-filled skull and opened his jaws.

"Wait! Please, don't . . . ," began Dinkin.

BONES

Bones in the human body: 206
Bones mixed up together: 412
Bones put together in the wrong order: 32

"YOOOOW!" yelled the skeleton, and he
started hopping around on one foot! Dinkin
and Edgar looked down. It was Herbert—he'd
sleep-eaten the skeleton's big toe! The
skeleton stumbled back into
the monster, knocking
them both back down
the stairs! The
skeleton flung
Dinkin and
Edgar into the
air as he fell!

"**YAAH!**" screamed Dinkin as he soared through the air. He reached out in a panic, grabbing the lampshade that hung from the ceiling at the top of the stairs. As he held on for dear life, he looked down to see Edgar, the skeleton, and the monster tumble to the bottom of the stairs. The two skeletons smashed into pieces as they hit the floor, sending bones flying everywhere.

"Edgar!" cried Dinkin.

"DON'T JUST SIT THERE, YOU MINDLESS MONSTER!" cried the skeleton's head as the monster struggled to its feet. "PUT ME BACK TOGETHER!"

"Dinkin, save yourself! And me if possible," cried Edgar's head, hoping he wasn't about to be crushed under a giant, monstrous foot. Dinkin watched in horror as the monster tried to piece the skeletons back together. But it just wasn't sure what bones belonged to which Frightening Thing!

113

"WHAT ARE YOU WAITING FOR, YOU BRAINLESS BEAST?" bellowed the skeleton's helpless head as the monster tried desperately to reassemble it. "NO, THE KNEE BONE CONNECTS TO THE THIGH BONE! THAT'S NOT THE THIGH BONE! THAT'S NOT EVEN *MY* BONE!"

The monster roared in frustration and tried to squeeze the skeleton's head onto Edgar's body, and Edgar's onto the skeleton!

"NO, NO, NO! DOES THIS LOOK RIGHT TO YOU, YOU CLOTH-BRAINED CREATURE?" boomed the skeleton.

"Well, this is certainly easier than going to the gym," said Edgar, so impressed with his new, gigantic frame that he almost forgot to be terrified.

Finally, as the monster started to figure out what went where, Dinkin looked down at the floor. It was a painful, nerve-rattling drop to the top of the stairs, but the alternative was waiting around to be caught. Then, suddenly . . .

"Dinkin, look out behind you!" cried Edgar. Dinkin turned to see the ghost about to fire another blast of sleep-breath. Dinkin had no choice but to let go and hope he didn't break anything. But Edgar had already leaped into action! With his new, massive skeleton body, he raced up the stairs in seconds, catching Dinkin as he plummeted downward! Edgar put Dinkin safely down on the landing, but caught the full brunt of the ghost's breath. Poor, mismatched Edgar tumbled, unconscious, back down the stairs.

"Edgar!" screamed Dinkin as he scrambled to his feet. He watched in horror as the monster popped off Edgar's sleeping head and reunited the giant skeleton's head with its body.

"ABOUT TIME!" said the skeleton, clambering back up the stairs toward Dinkin. "LOOKS LIKE WE'RE BACK ON TRACK—SO YOU CAN REALLY SCREAM NOW, IF YOU'D LIKE."

"Th-thanks very much," squeaked Dinkin, and took a deep breath.

"AAAAAA-
AAAAAH!"

WHAT IS THAT SMELL?

Terror at 9,889 scariness pounds

After screaming his most terrified scream to date, Dinkin rushed into his room and slammed the door. Danger was huddled in the corner of the room, his teeth chattering with terror. "Well, don't just stand there— The *Actually* Frightening Things are right outside!" cried Dinkin, looking around for somewhere to hide. The only place big enough for both of them was the closet. He grabbed Danger and they both clambered inside and shut the door.

"Wha-what's that smell?" whispered

Danger, holding his nose.

"Shh!" whispered Dinkin. "That's just my Bully-B-Gone. Would you rather live with the smell, or go out there and face your *Actually Frightening Things?*"

"Live with the smell! Live with the smell!" whispered Danger. A second later, the bedroom door burst open. Dinkin heard the monster snarl loudly as it crashed into the room, followed by the bony creak of the skeleton's joints.

"COME OUT, COME OUT, WHEREVER YOU ARE," said the skeleton. "WE HAVEN'T FINISHED WITH YOU YET."

The monster roared in rage, and Dinkin heard his bed being thrown across the room.

"HEY! THAT NEARLY HIT ME!" shouted the skeleton, slapping the monster on the head. "IF YOU'RE GOING TO THROW THINGS, COULD YOU AT LEAST TRY TO AIM AWAY FROM—WAIT, DO YOU HEAR . . . IS THAT BREATHING?"

Dinkin and Danger held their breath. They waited for 5.3 seconds, but in their all-consuming terror, it felt like at least 6.4. Then:

TAP-TAP-TAP!

"BOO! FOUND YOU!" said the skeleton, pulling the closet door off its hinges. Without any warning, the closet was lifted into the air and tipped forward. Dinkin and Danger (and the entire contents of the closet) fell out onto the floor. Dinkin looked up to see the monster holding the closet in his claws and the skeleton and ghost looming over them.

KEEP
OUT

"WHAT FUN! TWO VICTIMS FOR THE PRICE OF ONE!" said the skeleton. "I THINK WE'RE GOING TO ENJOY IT IN THIS DIMENSION. IN FACT, I THINK WE MIGHT STAY FOREVER!"

The *Actually* Frightening Things burst into hideous laughter, but after a moment, the skeleton stopped laughing and began to shake. The monster dropped Dinkin's closet and turned an even greener shade of green, and the ghost began to whirl and churn queasily in the air.

"WHAT . . . IS THAT SMELL?" asked the skeleton.

"S-sorry, that's my Bully-B-Gone spray." whimpered Dinkin. "It's a b-bit stinky."

"IT'S WORSE THAN 'STINKY'!" cried the skeleton, falling to its knees. "IT SMELLS LIKE . . . LIKE

THE END OF THE WORLD!"

The monster roared in pain and collapsed against the wall, while the ghost's cloudy body began to thin out and fade into nothing!

"What's happening?" asked Danger.

"They don't look very good," said Dinkin. "What's made them—wait a minute . . ."

"The Bully-B-Gone!" cried Dinkin and Danger together.

"The bottle—it's in my pants! Help me look!" yelled Dinkin. He and Danger scrambled around in the pile of clothes as The *Actually* Frightening Things flailed in agony. Dinkin ducked as the monster's tail whipped over his head, and Danger ducked out of the way of an angry blast of sleeping gas! Then, finally, Danger lifted the pants out of the pile, and reached into the pocket.

"I've got it!" he cried, pulling out the bottle of Bully-B-Gone. He threw it to Dinkin, who (despite his fear of flying objects) managed to catch the bottle. He aimed it in the direction of The *Actually* Frightening Things.

"Be gone!" he shouted, and started spraying. Never in the history of spraying had anyone sprayed so desperately. He covered the skeleton, monster, and ghost in equal quantities of foul-smelling liquid, and as he did so, the monstrous Frightening Things began to change. In fact, they began to *shrink*.

"HELP US! WE'RE MELTING!" screeched the skeleton. "NO, IT'S WORSE! WE'RE BECOMING . . . UN-FRIGHTENING!"

The shrieks and roars of The *Actually* Frightening Things quickly faded into tiny squeaks as they continued to shrink and change but Dinkin didn't stop spraying until the bottle of Bully-B-Gone was empty. Finally, he and Danger were staring at three of the least scary creatures they had ever seen. They were plump, cheerful, and wide-eyed, and so small that they could hold them in their hands. In fact, they looked almost . . . cute.

"You did it! You made them un-frightening!" said Danger, leaning down to inspect the transformed Frightening Things.

"I did?" said Dinkin. He picked up the tiny monster in his hand and stroked its belly. It giggled and then let out a little burp. He shook his head in disbelief and stared at the empty bottle in his hand. "I am definitely making more of this."

THE IMPORTANCE OF BEING DINKIN

Temperature: 42.8°F
Outlook: overcast, light breeze,
impending dread

After checking on his mom and dad (who were still sleeping soundly, thanks to the ghost's sleeping breath), Dinkin and his dimensional double gathered The (equally unconscious) Frightening Things in his bedroom. They even managed to carry Arthur back upstairs after finding him floating dazedly around the garage. Then they did their best to clean up the house, but after several hours, it still looked like a tornado had hit it. Finally, as dawn began to break, they put the bathrobe-covered mirror back where it belonged.

"I still can't believe my Bully-B-Gone worked on your Frightening Things," said Dinkin as they tried to put the closet the right way up. "I wish it had that effect on Boris Wack."

"I'm sorry about all the trouble I got you into, Dinkin," said Danger. "And all this mess. What are you going to tell your mom and dad?"

"I'm going to tell them that The Frightening Things from Dimension 9 came out of my mirror and wrecked the house. What else would I tell them?" replied Dinkin. "So, do you think you're going to be okay with *your* Frightening Things now?"

"Better than okay! Actually, I think we might even end up being friends," answered Danger, scooping up the tiny skeleton, ghost, and monster in his hands.

Dinkin glanced at his dozing Frightening Things and smiled. "That'd be nice."

"Well, I'd better go. My dimension's

probably missing all my death defying, daring deeds," said Danger. "Bye, Dinkin. Maybe we'll meet up again sometime."

"Not if I can help it," mumbled Dinkin. He spotted the Hidden Danger Detection Glasses, somehow still intact on his table, and picked them up. He handed them to Danger and said, "Here, just in case you need a new pair. Be careful, though—they're supposed to detect danger, but as far as I can tell, all they do is make it impossible to see things clearly."

"Uh, thanks," said Danger, pulling the bathrobe off the mirror. He was about to step back into his dimension, when he paused.

"Just one question," he said. "What's it *really* like being scared of *everything*?"

Dinkin thought hard. Finally, he shrugged and said, "*Terrifying*."

Danger gave him a sympathetic smile, and then disappeared into the mirror.

Dinkin breathed a huge sigh of relief and threw his bathrobe back over the mirror. He couldn't risk opening the doorway to Dimension 9 ever again. He had to get rid of the mirror once and for all. In fact, he had to get rid of every mirror in the house. No, the street! No, the whole world! No one was safe as long as one mirror remained.

THiS WAS A JOB FOR THE FRiGHTENiNG THiNGS!

As soon as they woke up . . .